RIVAL HEARTS

SUITOR'S CROSSING: HEARTS COLLIDE

BOOK ONE

HALLIE BENNETT

I0619598

Searching for more obsessed heroes?
Check out the Mountain Men of
Suitor's Crossing series!

CHAPTER ONE

SIERRA KIPLEY

"**I**'m blaming you if we end up in jail." My best friend and current accomplice hisses as we creep through the back door of Brewed.

"Relax. We're not getting caught, so we're not going to jail." I cross my fingers and hope that's true because being found snooping through Suitor's Crossing's favorite coffee shop, which also happens to be owned by my arch nemesis, would be terrible for my image as the local bakery owner. My mugshot on the front page of the *Suitor's Gazette* with the bold headline "Baking Bad: Local Baker is Toast" has me sending up an extra prayer for good luck.

A criminal record is *not* what my business needs right now.

After replacing the silver key on top of the doorframe, I quietly close the door and mentally pat myself on the back for finding Caleb's not-so-secret hiding spot. Our first obstacle was figuring out how to actually get into a locked Brewed, but the discovery of the key made it easy enough and negated the use of the tools I brought. *Slim credit card. One of those thin metal picks for turnlocks.* I'm no cat burglar, but I've seen enough movies to learn a thing or two.

Which explains my whole get-up from the tool kit to my outfit.

Black attire molds to my body in an attempt to be as sneaky as possible, and to live out my Bond girl dreams, though I doubt Sheriff Lawson will accept that as an excuse for why I'm scoping out Brewed after hours.

But I've got to know what the heck Caleb is up to over here.

Especially since a new chain restaurant opened its doors six months ago. A familiar chain that combines both of our specialties—coffee and pastries—into one easy location, efficiently cutting into our businesses. At first, I denied their impact, but as each month passed, the bakery numbers didn't lie. There was a steady decline. Nothing drastic that made me fear shutting down in the next few months, but enough of a change to raise concerns for a sustainable future.

Caleb let it slip that he had a plan to combat our latest competitor while bragging about his updated pecan braid recipe.

I rolled my eyes at the implication then just like I do now at the memory. As if Caleb's pastries have ever surpassed mine. No matter how many adjustments he makes to his recipes, he's not going to beat a nationally known chain either by upping his pastry game. No, he's got something else planned. I just have to figure out what. Which is why I'm bent over and tip-toeing through Brewed like an international jewel thief.

"Cole is going to kill me for doing this. *After* he laughs his ass off," Shannon mutters from behind me. Her husband and Caleb are pals, so it doesn't surprise me that he'd disapprove of his wife's late night shenanigans. But tough luck. Shannon was my best friend long before she married Cole, so my needs take precedence.

It's simple girl code.

"Stop worrying about Cole and start looking for—" To be honest, I'm not sure what I'm expecting to find. A binder full of schematics? A dossier of dirt to halt the rising popularity of the chain shop?

"Your dignity, perhaps?" Lights flash overhead and blind me for a second. Blinking in shock, I see Caleb standing by the light panel, arms crossed over his chest, and an annoying smirk twisting his handsome features. "*Tsk, tsk*, Sierra Bear. You've got some explaining to do."

Ugh! I hate his nickname for me. And I hate that he caught me snooping around his cafe.

Shannon groans behind me as red and blue lights paint me in the colors of my future—a convicted felon with nothing to show for it.

Is breaking and entering a felony if you didn't have a chance to take anything yet?

CHAPTER TWO

CALEB VICKERS

"You called the cops on me?"

"I didn't do anything, sweetheart. There's a silent alarm that automatically notifies the police department of a break-in," I explain, eyeing Sierra's skintight outfit. It screams *sexy Catwoman*, if Catwoman had large tits and an ass made for bouncing while riding my cock.

Shit. Time to shake that image out of my head.

I thought I was over my infatuation with my next door neighbor/bane of my existence, Sierra Kipley. From the moment we met at a Chamber of Commerce meeting, sparks flew. Not *heart sparks*, mind you, just your regular old run-of-the mill fireworks. My one-track mind had hoped they would translate to hot sex, but it immediately became apparent Sierra had other ideas.

Like electing me as her sworn enemy.

At least, that's what it felt like with every glare in my direction.

So, I played along. If she wanted a fight, then game on. Thus began the Cold Coffee and Cakes War as coined by my best friend's wife, who also happens to be Sierra's best friend. And who currently stood in my cafe looking ready to melt to the floor in embarrassment due to Sierra's crazy antics.

"Is everything alright down here?" A new voice enters the fray as a couple cautiously makes their presence known. James and Shiloh, who live above Sierra's bakery, come in from the hall that runs along the back of the building, allowing our two businesses and the empty storefront on the other side of Buttercream Dreams access to each other. James has a key to the back door in case of emergencies, so the flashing lights must have disturbed their evening.

"Yep, just have a minor case of B & E from our dear friend Sierra here." She rolls her eyes, and I can't help but smirk at her attitude. What did she expect to accomplish by sneaking into the cafe? I'm not really upset, and it's not like I think she's going to steal from me. But I do wonder what was going through her head.

"Sierra?" Shiloh's brows reach her hairline as she takes in the odd tableau. Two women dressed like extras in a spy movie. Sheriff Lawson stepping through the front entry. Multi-colored lights beaming across the space in a rhythmic pattern.

It's a fucking circus at two in the morning.

Sierra waves awkwardly and offers a chagrined smile. Poor Shannon's in the background, avoiding eye contact with everyone. Cole's going to have a field day when he learns what his wife has been up to.

"If everything's alright here, I'm going to head back out," Sheriff Lawson says. We all know each other, so it's obvious his authority won't be necessary. I'm not having Sierra arrested. I'll deal with her antics myself. *Privately.*

"Sure, thanks for getting here so quickly."

He shrugs. "It's my job." Then he turns to Sierra. "Avoid doing anything like this in the future, huh?"

She nods, a red blush creeping up her cheeks.

"I'm gonna take that as our cue to go, too. I'm glad everything's okay." James and Shiloh escape back upstairs, and Shannon excuses herself as well—ignoring Sierra's pleading expression for her not to leave.

I'm happy to have everybody clear out. We need to talk without an audience.

"Care to explain what you're really doing here?" I ask, going behind the counter to grab a couple of bottles of water. It's too late—*early?*—to make coffee.

"I don't have a good explanation," Sierra says. She slides onto a stool at the end of the counter before dropping her forehead to the linoleum between her crossed arms with a groan.

"Oh, I know that. Do you want me to guess what I think your purpose was?" This whole time I've been wracking my brain for an explanation of her behavior when it finally hit me. "You overheard me mention a plan to beat the new competition, so you thought you would sneak in and see what you could find. Am I close?"

"Are you psychic?" The words are garbled from where her face is still buried in her arms.

"No, I just happen to know you, babe. You're very predictable."

"Excuse me?" She straightens with a huff, and I hold back a chuckle at the red mark on her forehead. "Would a predictable person be in my current situation? I think not."

Bracing myself on the other side of the countertop, I twist the cap of her water bottle free before setting it in front of her. My finger lightly taps the flushed spot leftover from banging her head on the counter before she swats it away.

"Maybe they wouldn't resort to criminal activity, but I figured you'd try to learn my plan. My money was on you badgering Shannon for what she knows from Cole. Guess I'm too irresistible, though, and you had to go straight to the source."

"Ha! Don't flatter yourself." Her eyes flicker to the menu board behind me. "Shannon didn't know anything. Cole's lips were zipped tighter than a nun's chastity belt."

There's no disguising my bark of laughter for what it is—pure amusement at her hijinks. "Fuck, Sierra, you can be a real menace, you know that?" *Unfortunately, it seems that's my type.* "I warned Cole not to share with Shannon because this is between you and me. This conversation was supposed to happen at a reasonable hour when you decided to hound me for answers, but kudos to you for choosing breaking and entering over coming by for a civilized chat."

Sierra's gaze narrows, the deep green nearly eclipsed by her pupils. "Are you saying that you would have told me your grand plan if I'd asked?"

"Yep." I grin at her snort of disbelief. "Because you're a key part of it. Our feud is well-known in town, so I've been thinking... Why don't we put this conflict between us to our advantage and stick it to the *Chain That Shall Not Be Named*?"

"What do you mean?"

Grabbing a folder from underneath the counter, I lay it open for her. It's full of brainstorming sessions for what's been on my mind the last three weeks. "Let's have a competition. Your bakery versus my coffee shop. We'll drum up business while adding an element of fun for the town. It's not a secret how you feel about me, and this gives everyone a front row seat to the fireworks."

She thumbs through the sheets of paper, every once in a while releasing a low hum of interest or biting her lip in thought. Her emotions have always been a distraction for me. They're just so open and honest. What you see with Sierra is what you get. She doesn't hide.

It makes me wonder how she looks in bed while her curvy body's being railed by a—

"This isn't a totally terrible idea," she says reluctantly, snapping me out of my wayward thoughts. Clearly, the late hour is fucking with my head and loosening the reins around my inappropriate fascination with Sierra. "What are you thinking as far as contests? A list this long would be impossible to get through." She holds up the numbered lines of ideas that span one sheet front to back.

"You're right. I narrowed it down to three rounds. Sort of like a bake-off but with coffee thrown in. Those have stars next to them." I point out the blue doodles in the margins. "We can brainstorm more ideas tomorrow if those don't work. *After* we've gotten some sleep." The clock on the wall across from us shows that it's nearly 3 A.M. At the rate my mind is devolving into sexual fantasies featuring the one woman in town who absolutely despises me, it's time to wrap this up before I do something I'll regret. Like drag her across the counter and claim her sassy mouth for my own.

"Sounds good. Though I won't be getting much sleep since the bakery opens in a few hours." A black-gloved hand covers a yawn, reminding me of why we're even in this predicament, before she starts to back out the way she snuck in.

"You realize you can just walk out the front door, right? There's no point in sneaking around now."

"Right." She flushes. Plastic crunches beneath the flexing fingers around her half-empty water bottle. "Except I'm parked out back and don't fancy a walk around the block to get there. I'll see you tomorrow."

"Hang on, I'll walk you out." Suitor's Crossing is a safe town, but you can never be too careful. After securing the back door, we silently tread down the short hallway to the building exit, fatigue finally winning out over the adrenaline of earlier.

Sierra slips into her Nissan with a mumbled good-bye before reversing then slowly driving down the dark alley leading to the street. Sighing, I scrub a hand over my tired eyes then retrace my steps to get to my car in front of Brewed. It's a haphazard parking job considering I rushed over here once my phone alerted me to a break-in. Normally, I would've waited for a call from the cops rather than risking my life by confronting a thief or vandal, but the security camera trained on the back door showed an easily recognizable Sierra and Shannon.

And that was all I needed to jump out of bed and hightail it down to Main Street.

Wouldn't Sierra laugh if she knew how tightly she has me on a string...

CHAPTER THREE

SIERRA

"READY, SWEETCAKES? Doors open in ten minutes for the first round of the contest, and it looks like we've already got lines forming. Spreading the word on the Suitor's Crossing social pages was a stroke of genius."

"Don't sound so surprised." It's 7 A.M. on a Monday, and I've never had a line of customers waiting for me to open. Suitor's Crossing is a small town and staunch supporters of local businesses, but we're not exactly a hub for corporate suits in need of a caffeine hit before heading to the boardroom.

My busiest hours are actually after the morning school drop-off and right before the businesses around me open up at 9 A.M.

"*The Cafe Clash*. First round: Dough & Joe Duel," Caleb says, referencing the names we came up with for our contest and rounds. I figured we needed something catchy to make this thing feel like a real event for the town rather than a weird string of challenges between me and Caleb. Because this is for more than settling a personal score. It's about promoting our businesses so a big corporation doesn't win.

"Remember the rules? Whoever attracts the most customers during today's morning rush wins this round." This is the most equitable challenge as the other two skew towards either baking or brewing specifically.

It took us a day to sort out the details of the contest then another two weeks to hype it up around town. All of our friends shared it with their customers—like the engaged women who see Shannon for their wedding dresses at Blushing Brides Boutique or the groups of people who frequent Austin's bar The Ole Aces. Word spread quickly about *The Cafe Clash*, so I'm hopeful this brief truce Caleb and I have will prove fruitful.

"Yeah, yeah, yeah... *Don't cite the deep magic to me, Witch. I was there when it was written.*" His voice lowers to quote Aslan from *The Chronicles of Narnia*, prompting me to playfully smack his shoulder.

"You're such a child." An arrogant grin showcases his deep dimples, and I studiously ignore the little flutter they set off in my belly. So my arch nemesis is funny and attractive.

Like Paul Rudd mixed with Henry Cavill hot.

So what?

Just because I'm woman enough to objectively recognize his handsomeness doesn't mean anything. It's a natural response to a good looking man. Like if I saw a pair of bear cubs playing in the forests that surround Suitor's Crossing and felt the urge to touch all that cuteness. Doesn't mean I'd act on the impulse. I'm not stupid. I'd just admire from afar, knowing that getting any closer poses a clear danger.

Or in Caleb's case, a clear conflict of interest.

Because he's the man determined to steal my customers and run me out of business with the combination of his specialty coffee and inferior pastries.

CHAPTER FOUR

CALEB

When six o'clock rolls around, Sierra marches into Brewed with Mandy not far behind her. They wear matching expressions of frustration as both women join me at the back of the cafe where the announcement of today's winner will take place. Since Brewed stays open later than Buttercream Dreams, it made sense to have the conclusion of our first round here, with a declaration of the winner and encouragement for everyone present to attend our next event, Pastry Palooza, two days from now on Wednesday.

"Caleb."

"Sierra." I mimic her derisive tone, though it's difficult to mask my amusement. She's clearly pissed about my decision to use her muffins for my own benefit, but I couldn't resist the temptation. Teasing her is practically my side hustle because it's fun and Sierra makes it way too easy.

"Welcome everyone to *The Cafe Clash*!" James smiles and waves at a few latecomers. We chose an impartial party—McCoy Security—to handle tabulations and judging for the contest. As part of the family that owns the security firm and a military veteran, James McCoy is a popular man in Suitor's Crossing and the perfect person to ensure nothing is rigged in anyone's favor.

Not that this event is supposed to be anything but a fun way to increase visibility and profits for the bakery and coffee shop.

The overall winner gets bragging rights, but that's it. Otherwise, both Sierra and I come out victorious.

"Thank you for celebrating the Dough & Joe Duel with us. I hope everyone enjoyed the delicious treats and drinks offered today. I know I did." James pats his flat stomach, causing everyone to laugh. Raising a white envelope in the air, he motions for the crowd to quiet down. "Here are the results for today's winner. They'll have a leg up going into the next challenge—Pastry Palooza—on Wednesday. And the winner is... Brewed by a margin of seven! Congratulations to Caleb and his staff!"

Huh, that was closer than I thought it would be after my strong push at the end of the day.

Not that Buttercream Dreams is a slouch. Sierra works her ass off over there, and it shows. But her morning rush must have been crazier than I anticipated for the numbers to be so close.

"Congrats." Sierra offers her hand in a show of good sportsmanship.

Lightly squeezing her palm, I hold on for a second longer than necessary before letting go, enjoying the zap of sparks shooting from the spot of contact. "Thanks, it seems my gamble paid off."

"You mean the one where you filched my muffins for yourself?"

"*Filched* implies that I stole them when we both know I paid for them fair and square. So... you're welcome?" I slather a thick layer of smugness over my face before sliding behind the front counter and grabbing a to-go cup. A scoop of ice gets tossed in, then hazelnut, caramel, caramel cold brew, and healthy doses of cream and sugar. Three swishes of a metal spoon and it's good to go with a lid popped on top.

"For you." I set the iced coffee in front of Sierra. "A consolation prize."

She takes one hesitant sip, green eyes full of suspicion. "How do you know how I take my coffee?"

Not too difficult when I'm fucking obsessed with everything you do.

Wrong! I'm breaking myself of that habit.

Trying to anyway.

"Shannon stops by every morning for her vanilla latte, Willow's Americano, and your hazelnut caramel double shot."

"That could be for anyone."

"Nah, only one person I know prefers something that sweet—the fiery little baker next door who's mayor of Sugar Mountain." Plus, we write customer names on the cups to keep everything straight, but I guessed it was for Sierra long before Shannon mentioned it.

"Flattery will get you nowhere. Especially after the stunt you pulled today with the muffins."

"Does that mean our date is off tomorrow?" My bottom lip juts out in an exaggerated pout as I cross my arms on the counter and lean closer. For Pastry Palooza, we each have to create a treat inspired by Suitor's Crossing, and since Sierra has an industrial-sized kitchen, she agreed we could both share quarters while preparing for Wednesday's event.

Her gaze narrows. "It's not a date. I should ban you from the premises, but I prefer to win fair and square. Lord knows you haven't the slightest chance to beat me with anything baked in your tiny kitchen." She tilts her head toward the swinging door that leads to the small galley where our limited baked goods are made.

"Game on, sweetcakes."

THE BUTTERCREAM DREAMS stainless steel counter looks like the before shot of a baking competition show with boxes, bowls, and two standing mixers. Everything is laid out neatly and waiting to be turned into a winning recipe for tomorrow's Pastry Palooza.

"Quite the set-up, Sierra Bear." I palm some chopped pecans from a glass ramekin and pop them in my mouth.

She slaps my hand when I reach for more. "Paws off the nuts. I divided everything into separate stations: the base ingredients, fruits, candies, and salty add-ons. You didn't give me a list of anything specific you'd need, so hopefully, you can work with what I've got."

"Don't worry, I'm a professional. I can make anything work."

"Spoken like a true fan of *Iron Chef*. Maybe we should've chosen a special ingredient to base our recipes on in conjunction with the Suitor's Crossing theme." The reference to *Iron Chef* throws me for a loop. That's one of my favorite shows, and I constantly play reruns of various chefs going head to head in competition.

Maybe that's what subconsciously inspired The Cafe Clash...

"If the town had a signature ingredient, we probably would've thought of that, but since it doesn't..." I shrug. "Looks like we'll have to stick with our original plan. A pastry inspired by the town." Catching the apron Sierra tosses at me, I tie the strings around my waist before grabbing what I need for my tarts.

A companionable silence falls between us as we start working, and it's nice not having the usual tension hanging in the air. Baking may not be my strongest skill, but it seems like its soothing qualities of measuring and mixing calms both of us as I notice the relaxed slant of Sierra's shoulders and her quiet humming.

"So, *Iron Chef*. That's a throwback."

Sierra rolls out a ball of dough, sparing a glance my way before focusing on the slow glide of the rolling pin. "My mom and I used to watch it every Sunday night. She was obsessed with Bobby Flay."

"And you?"

"Hardly, I'm more of an Alton Brown fan."

"Like the nerdy type, do you?" I tease, although a part of me catalogs how very *not* nerdy I am. I don't wear the signature glasses. I'm not particularly savvy on a scientific subject—none of the stereotypical nerd qualities. Truthfully, I lean more towards hipster lumberjack with plaid flannels and jeans that fit properly, along with the occasional beanie.

"Competency, intelligence. Those are my kryptonite," Sierra says with a smirk as if I don't embody those things.

"I'm extremely competent at making the finest cup of coffee you'll ever drink. It takes a certain intelligence to create the perfect roast."

"Does it?" A smile hides in the corners of her mouth. My goal is to make her laugh because she doesn't do that enough around me.

"Come on, tell me you've had a better caramel double shot than the one I made for you yesterday."

"Fine, you know how to make a cup of coffee. But the way to a girl's heart isn't through her stomach, contrary to her male counterpart."

"Who's talking about hearts, sweetcakes?" Twin spots of red appear on her cheeks. She pushes a little harder on the rolling pin until the dough beneath spreads too thin and tears from the extra force.

"Damn it," she mutters.

Good to know I affect her as much as she does me.

"If the way to a girl's heart isn't through her stomach, then what is the way?" I ask, curious about her answer. I've known Sierra for a couple of years now, and I've never seen her date. A good thing, too, because it'd probably send me into an early heart attack from all the shock and jealousy. Okay, maybe it would give me minor heart palpitations. Because I swear I'm getting better with this obsession I have for her.

"Through her mind, *duh*. Women want to be wooed," she states matter-of-factly. "There's also the fact that the brain is actually your biggest sex organ—" Sierra pauses as if she can't believe she said that out loud. "Um... forget I just... uh... What are you making?" She fumbles over her words before completely dropping the topic.

"Smooth..." I laugh but allow the subject to change. We definitely shouldn't talk about sex. Not when just being near Sierra has my cock semi-hard and eager to fly into full mast. "An apple tart. I'm going for a nostalgic feel, especially since we have the apple orchard at the edge of town. You?"

"Cinnamon bacon scones. It's a play on *heart sparks* with the spice."

"Nice." Silence reigns supreme again, until we transport our goods to the ovens.

Sierra sets the timer, then leans back against the messy counter with a sigh. "This is going to be a nightmare to clean up." The back of her hand swipes across her forehead as her weary gaze studies the work to be done. Her picture-perfect set-up now lies in ruins with half-empty ramekins and flecks of sugar and flour decorating the counter.

"Cleaning will be easier with the two of us, though."

I reach for a folded rag when powdered sugar catches my eye. Fluffy. White. Openly available. An idea tickles my brain at the sight, and I can't resist my next move. Casually pinching the sugar between my fingertips, I flick it at Sierra, where it lands on her chest.

There's a pause.

Then an adorable growl.

"What was that?"

"What?" I ask innocently, fingers walking across the table in search of more ammunition.

"We are *not* having a food fight in my kitchen."

I flick brown sugar at her this time. "Who said we're fighting?"

"Seriously?" She brushes at the sprinkles of white and brown on her apron, but the sugar just smears. "And you called *me* a menace." Reaching forward, she grabs a handful of blue sprinkles and tosses them at my face. I duck but feel the little pellets hit my ear and the top of my head.

That's my girl.

"Oh, it's on now!" Tucking a bag of flour against my chest, I dodge a second onslaught of sprinkles before sending flares of flour cascading over Sierra's head.

Sprinkles, nuts, flour, sugar. It all flies through the air to coat every square inch of our bodies, until both of us are heaving with laughter, slumped on the floor in a truce.

"Well, if it wasn't a nightmare to clean before, now it definitely is." Sierra giggles, her chest heaving from exertion, and I wish the vee of her shirt dipped a little lower, so I could follow the map of baking products decorating her cleavage.

"Nightmare on Treat Street," I bite out—trying to keep things light and professional rather than turning the conversation back to sex and learning exactly how sweet Sierra tastes.

"Oh my gosh, you did not just say that." She lightly punches my shoulder, and it occurs to me that for someone who purportedly doesn't like me, Sierra touches me an awful lot. Sure, they're mostly annoyed slaps or shoves, but like a kindergartner who can't voice their crush, it's the equivalent of me pulling on her hair to get her attention.

"What? You've got to love a good rhyme."

"Obviously, I named my bakery Buttercream Dreams." Her head rolls against the cabinet behind us until her nose nearly brushes mine. Surprise lights within her features at our sudden proximity. We're sitting close, our faces inches apart. Flour clings to the wisps of hair that escaped her braid, and my stupid self immediately finds it endearing and sexy as hell.

"The timer should go off soon," she whispers, confusion shining in her eyes as they flick from mine down to my mouth. *Or maybe that's wishful thinking.*

Leaning closer, I wonder what she'd do if I kissed her right now. Maybe the animosity she's held against me all these years will transform into passion. Desire. "Sierra..." I feel the softest caress of her lips on mine, before the timer dings, and she jerks back.

"Oh, we better get that. We don't want them to burn." Hopping to her feet, Sierra grabs mittens to pull out the hot trays, and I bang my head back against the cabinet in frustration.

Thwarted by the damn Pastry Palooza.

CHAPTER FIVE

SIERRA

"Stupid, stupid, stupid... What were you thinking?"

"Are you talking to yourself again?" Mandy's amused question breaks into my litany of insults. It's not unusual for me to get lost in my own little world while working and start talking aloud.

Repeating a task I don't want to forget.

Mumbling encouragement to croissants to be extra fluffy.

Odd stuff like that.

When I'm caught, mostly by Mandy since she's my right hand woman, we laugh it off before returning to work. This time, however, I can't bring myself to find the humor in the subject that's prompted my latest musings.

Caleb and that almost kiss.

What the hell were you thinking?

"Hey, is everything alright?" Mandy peers around my shoulder as if the answer to my silence lies within the cupcakes I'm currently frosting for a PTA meeting tonight.

"Yes. No. I don't know." Is it *alright* that I almost kissed my arch nemesis last night? Is it *alright* if I forgot we're supposed to be mortal enemies because he's so damn hot and hilarious? The answers to those questions continue to elude me, thus my muttering to these poor cupcakes.

"What's going on?" Mandy may work for me, but she's also my friend. And she knows better than anyone, except for Shannon, my feelings about *him*.

Still, I bite my lip, debating whether I should tell her about my lapse in judgment or not. *What the hell?* Maybe she can set me back on the straight and narrow. "Caleb and I almost kissed."

"Whoa." The stack of clean bowls she was about to put away clatters on the table. "Are you serious? When? Last night when you were baking together?"

"Yep." The SCHS I'm attempting to pipe on top of the cupcakes looks like a red blob instead of the school's initials. Huffing in annoyance, I scrape the shoddy lettering off and try again.

"Interesting." Mandy's elbows rest on the tabletop as her brows furrow in contemplation. Since I knew this large school order was due today, I had one of our part-timers come in to man the front of the bakery, which means the two of us are free to chat. *Or shake some sense into me.* Whichever works.

"What does that mean? *Interesting.* Sounds like a scientist observing the mating habits of ants for the first time."

"*The mating habits of*—" She slashes her hand through the air. "You know what? That's not the point. The point is that it kind of makes sense to me. This thing between you and Caleb. For years, you've had this rivalry going, but now that you're working together, it's not too much of a leap for the tension to be attraction rather than dislike."

"Okay, Dr. Phil." I roll my eyes at the psychoanalysis, but the unhinged part is that I'm not sure she's wrong. I've always found Caleb attractive. But his other attributes—AKA being my neighboring competitor for the breakfast crowd—have always overshadowed those feelings.

Until now.

Because Caleb is exciting.

Spontaneous.

The little food fight we had last night was the most fun I've had in forever, even if it *was* a pain to clean. I'm not some uptight hermit, but the weight of knowing my business could eventually be in trouble due to the arrival of chain restaurants has put a damper on my mood lately.

Except for when Caleb is around.

"I'm just calling it like I see it," Mandy says, plucking one of the piping bags from the table to help me frost the remaining dozens of cupcakes I have left.

"You didn't see anything," I point out.

"I may not have been a witness to this *almost kiss*, but I've seen the way Caleb looks at you when he doesn't think you'll notice."

"Oh, and you're just now telling me about this?" What are we? Rapunzel and Flynn Rider from *Tangled*?

Okay, but that would actually be awesome.

"I didn't think it mattered because there was no way in hell you were giving him a chance. He's your *arch nemesis*, remember?" She uses air quotes this time. "But he does tend to stare whenever you're around. I think you've kept this feud going for longer than he would have, and he's just along for the ride."

"Geez, you're full of revelations today, aren't you?"

"I had therapy this morning." She winks right as Keely comes back asking for some help up front.

"Be there in a sec!" Mandy heads that way with one last parting shot. "For the record, I don't think there's anything wrong with liking Caleb. Aside from the whole muffin thing—" she grins "—he's actually a good guy, and he hasn't really done anything to trash your business."

She has a point.

The chain restaurant has done more damage in the past six months than Caleb ever did in three years. "Thanks for the chat. Now go help Keely."

"Aye aye, boss." Mandy salutes me, then disappears through the swinging door separating the kitchen and the front.

There's nothing wrong with you liking Caleb. That's what she said, but I'm not sure I believe it. Not sure I'm ready to pull a one-eighty on everything I've thought for the past few years.

"Once I get through this competition," I tell myself. "I'll deal with whatever I'm feeling.

Until then, I've got a contest to win.

Starting with tonight's event: Pastry Palooza.

CHAPTER SIX

CALEB

AFTER ADDING THE CUSTOMER opinion to the votes of the three judges from McCoy Security, James announced Buttercream Dreams as the winner of Pastry Palooza half an hour ago, so there's been a nonstop line of congratulations to Sierra.

Her victory isn't a total surprise, considering I'm well aware of how much everyone loves her baking. Hell, I'm part of that crowd myself—not that I'd ever tell her, at least not while we're in the midst of a competition.

But I'm not bitter about her win, and with the chaos of the day finally winding down, it's time to enact my hastily cobbled together plan. Sierra and I have been working nonstop for *The Cafe Clash*, so I figure we're owed a little bit of a reprieve.

Especially after our almost kiss.

It was the perfect hammer to shatter the flimsy walls containing my attraction. Now it's impossible to keep my feelings in check. Sierra is business smart and curvy with a sassy sense of humor. How the hell am I supposed to resist?

The answer is I'm not.

"Come on, let's get out of here." I tug on her arm after the last of the stragglers disappear.

"Yeah, I should get back to perfecting my Suitor's Crossing inspired latte," she says, her eyes glued to the screen of her phone. "Then post about the Brew Battle—"

"On the town's socials. I know, I know. But they can wait. Come on."

Sierra reluctantly follows me outside to my Jeep Cherokee. It's 6:30 PM on a Wednesday, so Main Street is practically deserted except for the spaces in front of Brewed and Daffodil's—a local restaurant that eschews the usual 5 PM closing time of its neighbors. Turning into Suitor's Crossing's lone parking garage, a three-story concrete structure next to the bank, we slowly ascend the spiral of parkings spots until we reach the top.

"Your idea for a break is hanging out in a parking garage?" A bubble of laughter fills the vehicle as Sierra searches for the punchline. She twists in her seat, surveying the empty square of concrete around us.

"Trust the process," I say, mentally crossing my fingers that I haven't fucked this up already. When the idea first came to mind, it sounded romantic—an excellent way to woo Sierra since I took that conversation we had to heart. But now I'm not so sure. An empty parking garage might read as *crazy serial killer* more than *romantic suitor*.

Too late to back out now.

I reverse into a space at the western edge of the lot. A rooftop view of Main Street lies below us as the sun hovers above the horizon, and the mid-March breeze is just cool enough to warrant the extra blankets I brought.

The passenger door slams shut, then Sierra rounds the rear of the car to watch me open the back hatch and reveal folded blankets, a battery-operated lantern, and a red cooler.

"What is all of this?"

"What's it look like, sweetcakes? We're having a picnic for dinner."

"A picnic," she deadpans. Disbelief wrinkles her brows as I shake out a blanket and lay it out on the Jeep carpet.

Patting the spot, I tilt my head for her to get inside. "Up and at'em. We're tailgating while enjoying the sunset."

"You're serious." She bites her lip and looks between me and the back of my Jeep. "Is this some kind of mind game before the last round of competition? Because I don't understand what the heck is going on."

My hand gently pushes Sierra toward the picnic setup. Of course, she's hesitant and confused. This wouldn't be my Sierra if she didn't question my intentions at least once a day.

"I'm wooing you," I admit. I hadn't planned on laying it all on the line tonight. My strategy was to warm her up to me, capitalize on how well we've worked together on *The Cafe Clash*, then admit that I'd like us to be more than business rivals.

But it seems that ship has sailed since Sierra is skeptical as fuck.

"Wooing... *me*."

"Yup. Champagne?" The chilled bottle pulls easily from the ice in the cooler, and I quickly pop it open before pouring the bubbly liquid into two plastic cups. They're not the fanciest things around, but they'll do for a parking lot picnic.

Sierra accepts the cup then downs the contents in one swift gulp, offering it back to me for an immediate refill. Her bewildered gaze tracks my movements as I arrange food containers in the sliver of space between us in the Jeep. Our meal is basically a deconstructed charcuterie board—or an elevated Lunchable, depending on how you look at it—meats, cheeses, fruits, along with an assortment of crackers. All courtesy of Pickle & Rye, a local delicatessen.

Sierra slowly chews and swallows the stack of a pretzel cracker, provolone, and prosciutto I give her. "You need to explain to me why the hell you're *wooing* me. We've got mere weeks of being civil under our belt due to this contest. As if that isn't enough of a reason to keep things professional, there are years before that of total animosity. You don't like me; I don't like you. So, where is this coming from?"

"I've never disliked you, Sierra. And animosity isn't how I'd describe our relationship. It's a fun rivalry. I never truly wanted you to fail." I swallow my own double stack of capicola and colby jack. "I actually wanted to be friends, especially considering how our best friends are married to each other, but you've never seemed keen on the idea. Until now."

CHAPTER SEVEN

SIERRA

IS HE FOR REAL?

I feel like I'm in an episode of *The Twilight Zone*. Any moment a spaceship will appear on the horizon with a message from another planet admitting to infiltrating the human species, and Caleb is one of their alien hosts.

Because I don't know who this man is.

Granted, he's upended my previous impression of him by working with me to help both of our businesses succeed, but how am I supposed to jump from previous arch nemesis to potential boyfriend material?

Because I think that's what Caleb's alluding to.

This is a date.

He's wooing me.

And I'm flabbergasted.

Shannon's going to have a field day with this new development.

"Earth to Sierra." Caleb flicks my shoulder. "You still in there or have I managed to finally stump that clever brain of yours?"

I swat his hand away. "Knock it off. I'm just absorbing everything."

"I get it. It's a lot to take in. A dashingly handsome and absurdly charming guy like myself can be intimidating, but you're woman enough to handle me, Sierra Bear. I believe in you." He winks then chokes on the drink of champagne he just chugged when I bump his shoulder with mine. *Hard.*

"You are incorrigible. And think way too highly of yourself." Though a smile pulls on my cheeks at his antics. Caleb is silly, but then again, so am I. When I'm not stressed about work. I mean who else would cosplay as a Bond girl and break into their enemy's business?

"Don't pretend you don't love me. I keep you on your toes, sweetcakes."

"I gave up ballet when I was ten."

There's a pause, then Caleb's deep laughter rumbles from the Jeep, his broad shoulders shaking and head thrown back in amusement. Popping a grape into my mouth, I contemplate a future where the man next to me isn't my arch nemesis. Where he's my partner instead. A sexy, humor-filled partner that isn't out to fuck my business over but wants to fuck *me* instead.

"I didn't realize you were a dancer. Have you visited the new dance studio that opened up? One of the Reaper's Wolves' women runs it, I think."

"You're right. Amelie. I met her at a Chamber of Commerce meeting. But no, I haven't attended a class. I've been too busy keeping the bakery afloat."

"Has business really been that bad lately?" he asks, resting on an elbow at his side.

"Nah… It was just a joke." My chest rises with a long inhale. "Though it may become reality sooner rather than later, if the *Chain Who Shall Not Be Named* continues to cut into my customer base. Suitor's Crossing is loyal, but there's no denying the fact that a drive-through off the interstate is more convenient than stopping by my shop."

"Same could be said for Brewed, too." He lifts a hand to gently nudge my chin up. "Just means we've got to stay creative and join forces instead of dividing our resources by fighting each other *and* the big bad corporation."

"Sometimes you make too much sense," I grumble, crossing my arms over my chest. Bright orange and pink paint the sky as the sun continues to set, and a blast of wind raises goosebumps on my skin.

"Are you cold?" Caleb unfolds a blanket and drapes it over my lap, tucking the ends under my legs like I'm a burrito.

"Thanks, but this is ginormous. We can probably share." Now why did I suggest that? We don't need to cozy beneath one blanket together. "Actually, nevermind... That's a dumb idea."

Caleb shifts closer, wrapping an arm around my hips to drag me into his warm, muscular side. "*It's a brilliant, beyond brilliant idea.*"

"*Parent Trap*? Are you some kind of movie quote vault? Ready to spit out an appropriate line for any occasion?" The heat of his body seeps through my clothes as I focus on forming coherent sentences rather than relaxing into his embrace. An insurmountable feat, judging by the way my muscles immediately melt into him.

"Only with select films." Caleb's breath skims my temple, and I shiver, though I'm the furthest thing from chilled at the moment.

"Damn, you're still freezing?" He roughly rubs a palm over my thigh as if to get the blood pumping, but my hand quickly falls to stop the movement—right at the crease where my leg meets my overexcited pussy.

Swallowing the lump in my throat, I croak out some nonsense about the weather and body temperatures, except it's obvious that neither of us are listening because our hands haven't moved, our gazes locked on each other, waiting to see what happens next.

What do you want to happen next?

I flash back to last night's almost kiss and lick my dry lips. Scruff covers Caleb's chin and cheeks, highlighting his very kissable mouth. One that inches closer and closer until my lashes flutter shut with the first brush of his lips against mine.

"This okay, sweetcakes?" The murmured words vibrate between us as Caleb sticks to light, teasing kisses across my cheek and neck. My fingers tangle in his shaggy hair and scratch at his scalp.

"If it wasn't, then you'd be wheezing from a punch to your solar plexus," I manage to say through labored pants.

He chuckles. "My violent girl. Such a little spitfire." This time he claims my mouth with more force, gripping my chin between his fingers and angling me just the right way for his tongue to sweep in and steal my breath.

Good lord, the man can kiss.

And I'm in massive trouble.

CHAPTER EIGHT

SIERRA

PASTRY PALOOZA WAS a grand slam with everybody loving my cinnamon bacon scones. Unfortunately, that's where my luck seemed to run out because, despite the judges of McCoy Security appreciating my artistic latte art, when it came to taste for my Suitor's Crossing-inspired drink, Caleb won by a mile. And with two wins under his belt to my measly one, James declared him *The Cafe Clash* winner.

What a way to end the week.

On a freaking loss.

"Congratulations," I mutter half-heartedly, shaking Caleb's hand Friday evening as we pose for a picture in the town's newspaper. The sparks the touch ignites reminds me of our kiss in his Jeep. A kiss I've shoved to the back of my mind while I prepped for the Brew Battle, the last contest of our competition. But now that it's done—with Buttercream Dreams named the loser—I'm not sure how to feel about Caleb.

Do we go back to the way we were? Or do I take his suggestion and continue to work with him rather than by myself? And how does that work if we're dating?

Oh my god, I'm thinking about dating—and doing other pleasurable things—*with Caleb Vickers.*

"Don't sound so glum, Sierra Bear. We're all winners here, right?" Caleb grins. "Business has been booming for both of us. You can't deny that."

"No, but I hate losing, especially to you."

"Aww, come on... It's not so bad when you have a worthy opponent, right?"

"Sure." My eyes roll toward the ceiling as I smother a laugh. Always so confident. So cocky. Before all of this, that would have annoyed me. But now I find it kind of sexy.

Ugh, what happened to my resolve to ignore this attraction to him?

Probably disappeared around the time his hand cupped my breast during our make out session.

"You guys are amazing." Luna Fielding, a quirky local and multi-passionate entrepreneur, comes up to congratulate us with her husband in tow. Purple curls tickle my cheek as she gives me a hug. "I was just telling Austin how collaborating together has really worked for you guys. Everything you've created this past week has been next-level awesome."

"Thank you! That means a lot coming from you." And I mean it. Luna is a creative genius, whether it's building the dating app for town locals called Suitor's Sparks or taking on remodeling projects around town like Austin's office at The Ole Aces. Her stamp of approval makes me feel better about potentially working with Caleb again.

Speculation lights up Luna's eyes as she looks up at Austin before returning her attention to Caleb and I. "Have you guys thought about teaming up permanently?"

"What do you mean?" The question catches me off guard.

Team up permanently?

"Well, y'all work right next to each other," she says, ticking points off on her fingers. "It would be easy enough to remove this wall that separates the spaces and combine it into one incredible cafe with the best coffee *and* pastries." Luna's face sparkles with excitement. "I would help, of course, if it's something you're interested in. Oh! You could premiere the grand opening at the All Schools Day Parade! Tons of people will be in town, and there will be a lot of publicity for the event."

"That's not a bad idea."

"You want to remove a wall?"

Caleb and I speak at the same time, though he doesn't sound as shocked as I am at Luna's proposal.

"My girl's all about expansion and leveling up." Austin wraps an arm around Luna's shoulders before dropping a kiss to her head. "But I can vouch for her talent. The Ole Aces is better for her hand of magic."

Of course he'd say that. He's in love with her.

But I'm not.

And I'm not mentally prepared to completely change my entire business to work with Caleb. No matter how easy Luna makes it sound.

"He's being modest. Rhys and Austin already had most of the main bar area renovated. I swooped in at the last minute to add a couple touches to his office." Luna places a hand over her husband's heart, an adoring expression brightening her features. They really are a cute couple—the scarred veteran and curvy creative. "But it's just a thought. I want both of you to have as much success as possible, and if this event has shown me anything, it's that the two of you are a force to be reckoned with." She smiles to soften the blow of her suggestion.

But I can't shake it.

Even after she's gone.

Even after it's just Caleb and I left in Brewed to clean up the aftermath of *The Cafe Clash* ending.

"You've been suspiciously quiet all night. Still thinking about Luna's suggestion?"

Setting my broom against the wall, I face him. "Aren't you?"

"The idea has merit." He rests against the front counter, setting aside the rag and spray bottle he'd been using to wipe down the top.

"How can you say that? She wants us to basically disband our current businesses to create a super cafe." I pace the checkered floor as thoughts of what it would mean to team up with Caleb race through my mind. "I'm not sure I'm ready to give up Buttercream Dreams—the bakery I've worked for years to build. Can you say the same about Brewed?"

He sighs and runs a hand through his disheveled hair. The shaggy strands really do need a trim. Even if the longer length suits him. Tempts me to grab on and—*Not the time, Sierra!*

"Don't think about it as giving something up. Think about what you'll be gaining instead. Our core businesses will still be the same, whether it's Buttercream Dreams or Brewed or a different super cafe name," he jokes. "The benefit is growing our businesses in a direction that's more profitable, more sustainable. That's what this whole event was about, right? Combating the current state of affairs with *you know who* breathing down our necks."

He's not wrong.

And I hate that.

"What would we even name it? Brewed Buttercream Dreams?" *Bleh, not the catchiest name around.*

"Nah, that's too long. Plus, it clings to the old. We want to step into the future and a new beginning. I was thinking something like 'Cups and Cakes Crossing.'"

"You're kidding. You already thought of a name?"

"Wasn't that difficult. You know I like wordplay." He winks, and a mischievous grin shows off his dimples.

"Crossing's Cups & Cakes." I rearrange the words. Test them out.

"Even better. Then we're paying homage to the town which is bound to gain us major points."

"This is insane. You know that, right?"

Caleb straightens from his bent position. "Does that mean you're in?"

Does it? This is a major decision. Shouldn't I take longer than the few hours it's been since Luna first suggested the merger? Except this doesn't feel like a rash decision. It kind of feels like the next step in my career.

Am I really considering this?

"If Luna's planning on demolishing a wall, we're going to take a financial hit since we'll have to close down during the renovation."

"Good thing we just had this week of increased profits to tide us over." Caleb rounds the counter and stops my agitated pacing with two hands on my hips.

Staring up at his warm brown eyes, a thrill of anticipation runs through my veins. "Are you always this optimistic?"

"I have to be when you're always glass half empty."

"I haven't always been that way," I mutter, dropping my chin to avoid his gaze.

"Yeah, I know. That chain is really getting to you, aren't they?"

"They shouldn't. I'm not on my last leg or anything, business-wise."

"No, but you're thinking ahead. Trying to prevent any problems that might crop up in the future." He squeezes my love handles before hugging me closer. The comforting scent of coffee beans and something uniquely Caleb surrounds me like a cozy blanket on a cool winter's night.

"Look. I know this seems impulsive, and I won't deny that I have my misgivings. Hell, I've worked at least as hard as you building Brewed. But the fact of the matter is, no matter our egos, the both of us know that people come to me for coffee and you for pastries. They will literally stop by my place and then five minutes later walk over to yours. Why don't we get rid of the commute? Admit our weaknesses, and let each other's strengths compensate for the lack."

Why does he sound so reasonable? It makes it harder to convince myself that this might be a terrible idea.

"What do you say, Sierra Bear? We can call Luna right now. Have her start demoing the wall next week. That'll give us eight weeks until the All Schools Day Parade. Two months before our grand reveal. We can get a lot done in that time."

My skin itches with the prospect of a new adventure. Business hasn't exactly been stale the past few years, but the whirlwind of opening my own bakery and becoming profitable has died down. Do I really want to sacrifice the little bit of peace I've carved out for myself by jumping into an expansion by merging with Brewed?

My gut says *yes*.

So, I send a prayer heavenward and offer Caleb a tremulous smile before committing to an unknown future. "I'm in."

CHAPTER NINE

CALEB

After agreeing to join forces and become Crossing's Cups & Cakes, we wasted no time getting the ball rolling by setting up a meeting with the owner of our building and business leases, Mike Jones.

"Do you think he'll go for it? I mean we're asking him to approve a major renovation. Going from two leasing checks to one." Sierra nibbles her lip as I hold the door to Design Time open. Mike owns this embroidery and screen printing shop that also sells local sports memorabilia and keeps his office here for all meetings.

"We're adding value to his building by upgrading everything as we go. Plus, there's nothing stopping him from combining how much each of us pay into one lump sum each month, so he doesn't lose out on money."

"Hello! Welcome to Design Time," a woman emerges from the back of the retail space and shuffles behind the cash register in the middle of the store.

"Hi, I'm Sierra Kipley and this is Caleb Vickers. We have a two o'clock meeting with Mike."

"Oh, of course. He mentioned it earlier. You can follow me." She waves a hand toward a long conference table squeezed into a makeshift storage space. "I'm Avery, by the way. I'll let Mike know you're waiting."

We sink into two cushioned chairs and swivel to face the table. Mike joins us a few minutes later, and by tacit agreement, I launch into the plans Sierra and I have, pouring on the charm and enthusiasm in the hopes that our vision isn't dashed before it has a chance to take flight.

"I'm surprised to hear the two of you want to team up. Figured there'd be too much bad blood between the businesses." Mike steeples his fingers and reclines in his seat across from us.

"We've worked through our differences," Sierra assures him. "*The Cafe Clash* gave us an opportunity for some honest conversations that brought to light how unfair I was being to Caleb and vice versa."

"I see..."

The doorbell above the front door rings out, and Avery returns from a hall leading to the back of the building. Scooching closer to the table, Sierra and I try to give her room to squeeze behind us in the tight meeting space.

"I'd like to see the schematics before any demoing occurs. I need to ensure everything goes through the proper channels as far as building codes and licenses."

"Of course. We'll be happy to get those for you," I agree, my hand drifting to Sierra's thigh beneath the table and contracting around the soft flesh.

This is promising.

If Mike wants to see our plans for the new set-up, then that means his answer isn't an immediate no. That means he's considering our proposition, and we're one step closer to making Crossing's Cups & Cakes a reality.

Mike claps his hands in finality then rises to his feet. "Great, I'll look forward to those, and if everything checks out, then we can move on to discussing updated staff uniforms and any merchandise you want to sell." He grins and shakes both of our hands.

"You've got it. You guys did a great job with the employee aprons for Buttercream Dreams, so I don't see why we wouldn't hire Design Time again," Sierra says before we exit the store.

Rows of cars line the sidewalks of Main Street as we head toward Brewed. It's a bustling Tuesday with clear skies and the sun shining brightly over the colorful shop windows. A good omen for the beginning of our partnership.

Speaking of which...

"Are we going to tackle the elephant in the room yet?" I ask as we curve around a mom rubbing sunscreen on her toddler.

"What elephant?"

"You and me, sweetcakes." Daffodil's appears on our right, and I divert Sierra toward the entrance for a late lunch. "Don't think I've forgotten about our kiss."

Once we're seated, her dark brows scrunch together while she studies the laminated menu. As if she hasn't eaten here before and doesn't know exactly what she wants—strawberry poppyseed salad with chicken, one of Daffodil's spring specials. I remember hearing her complain to Shannon last June when the restaurant switched to summer-appropriate entrees, and she couldn't get it anymore.

"It's a moot point now. We can't date if we're business partners."

"Says who?"

"Literally every HR handbook that bans interoffice relationships. Every advice column that warns about mixing business with romance," Sierra drawls, shrugging beneath the pink cardigan covering her shoulders. She sips her iced tea with lemon, daring me to contradict those points.

"For every article and rule that frowns upon working romantic relationships, I guarantee there's a corresponding one that approves of them. Look at Austin and Luna. They worked together and fell in love. Do you think there's something wrong with their relationship?"

"The key word here is *worked* together. Past tense. They didn't become business partners. It was a contracted job that had a start and finish date, giving them freedom to pursue something more."

"So, we set boundaries." I'm not against a compromise. If that's what Sierra needs, then I'm happy to accommodate. What I won't agree to is keeping things strictly professional.

We've proven there's too much chemistry between us to stay objective. Sparks fly whenever we're near each other, and if those sparks don't have an outlet—like making out and fucking like a pair of horny teens—then it wouldn't surprise me if they shifted back to animosity. At least on Sierra's part.

"I'm listening... What kind of boundaries?" She moans in delight at the first bite of her salad, and I fidget in my seat, trying to inconspicuously adjust my hardening cock.

Don't get a boner in Daffodil's.

Don't get a boner in Daffodil's!

"Separation of church and state. As much as it's reasonable. That means no business talk outside the four walls of the cafe, and we keep it professional during business hours."

She hums in approval. "What happens if we break up? It won't be so easy to avoid each other when our finances are tangled together."

s   e agree now that whatever happens between us doesn't
a   he business. We're both adults. And even when you
      I was your arch nemesis, we maintained a cool civility,
      since Shannon and Cole are our friends. If a romantic
      ip ends, there will be a concerted effort to remain
      and amiable."

      chatter surrounds us. The clink of silverware
      ing each murmured conversation as Sierra continues
      contemplating my terms. I hope I don't have to push
      pe she wants me as much as I want her—and she
      compromise, willing to give us a chance.

      now, I never would have pegged you for the
      ne in a relationship," she finally says. "Especially
      propensity for diving into new things so quickly. But
      y persuasive. Every damn word out of your mouth
      h sense, I struggle to come up with a rebuttal." She
      me. "It's annoying as hell."

      sorry, sweetcakes." I finish the last of my potato
      a napkin across my mouth. "Just think of it as a
      e to love."

      A balled up straw wrapper bounces off my chest.
      vinced me. We'll try these boundaries, and see

      irl." Sierra blushes at the endearment, and now
      d that up, I can't resist rising a little out of my
      nd around her neck, and planting a hard kiss on

      ryone.

They'll know soon enough that the Cold Coffee and Cake War has officially ended, and the armistice was just sealed with a kiss.

CHAPTER TEN

SIERRA

Once we gave her the okay, Luna called her contractor friends over at Wilson-Covington Construction, who added us to their booked schedule as a favor to her, and the plan for Crossing's Cups & Cakes was put into motion.

"I'm really proud of you." Shannon sorts through a rack of wedding dresses in preparation for her next bridal appointment as I lounge on one of the overstuffed chairs meant for a bride's guests.

"Really? You don't think I'm making a huge mistake?"

"I think you've forgotten what it took for you to get to this point," she says, presenting a white mermaid-style dress before I shake my head in disapproval. "Calculated risks. Being a small business owner isn't for the faint of heart, and it's not for someone who wants to play it safe. Two things you definitely are not, despite this latest spat of self-doubt."

I sigh, banging my head against the back of the chair. She's right. I'm not an overly cautious person. I go for what I want. Make the tough decisions.

And risks are necessary for the vitality of a business.

When it comes to Buttercream Dreams, though, it's been my baby for years. It didn't pop out of thin air. I educated myself on the ins and outs of a bakery and learned from my mistakes.

I fought hard for my dream when the odds were stacked against me.

"I think it's just easier to worry about a choice I've already made versus thinking about the future and Caleb," I admit.

"Ah, procrastination. I'm well-acquainted with it." Shannon sinks into the chair next to mine and snags her teal water bottle for a drink. "But you're gonna have to face those pesky feelings eventually. Especially now that the two of you will be working together on a more permanent basis."

"Ugh, I know... But life was easier back when he was just my arch nemesis." Shannon laughs at the title like she's done a million times in the past. "Things were black and white. Caleb stole my customers. I returned the favor. He frustrated me, and I flustered him. Sympatico. *Sym-pat-i-co.*" Each syllable bursts from my mouth like a series of word bubbles waiting for someone to pop them.

"And now you two are k-i-s-s-i-n-g. *Kiss-ing,*" Shannon teases with a lift of her eyebrows.

"Yep..." And we have a date tonight.

I don't know if it counts as our second after the picnic or our first because it's *official*—like Caleb asked me out and everything. The number doesn't really matter, except for the part where my hormonal body wonders if it'll finally get a chance to experience the thick ridge I've caught bulging from Caleb's jeans lately.

Sex may not be the smartest action, considering how mired I am in the emotional swamp of my confusing feelings, but then again, maybe it'll clear my head. I could use some stress relief, and it's only fair that Caleb provides it since he's the man responsible for fucking with my head.

Here's to hoping he fucks with my pussy soon, instead.

"WHAT IS THIS PLACE?" I ask Caleb hours later after he parks in front of a large warehouse lit up with bright lights. The parking lot is full, and there's a big sign on the front that says Capstone Climbing and Adventure, but I'm not exactly sure what that means.

"We need to mix things up a little." Caleb grins before opening the driver's side door and rounding the Jeep to help me out. "Step out of our comfort zones and remember our boundaries—no shop talk for the rest of the night."

The warehouse entrance leads to a massive space filled with adult-sized activities. Like the wall lined with an indoor rock climbing wall, colorful handles decorating the fake stone. Then there's the supersized jungle gym that curves around the back of the building.

"This place is wild," I say, my wide eyes soaking in everything at once.

"Right? I've never been here before, but it sounded fun when I googled date ideas."

"You googled date ideas?" Why is that so charming? The vision of him hunched over his phone researching places to take me. It's freaking cute as hell.

"I'm wooing you, remember?" He gently taps my temple with his knuckle. "And trying out a new place together sounded like an adventure."

"You ever been rock climbing before?" Two people currently scale the floor to ceiling structure. Thirty feet above the ground, their twin athletic bodies bend and stretch for each handhold.

"Nope. You?"

"Do I seem like the type of girl who likes to climb rocks for fun?" He's lucky I'm not afraid of heights or else this would be a total bust.

"You never know." He shrugs then guides me to the welcome counter where a guy stands chatting to another employee. After paying the adventure fee, Caleb and I follow the guy to the rock wall where he gives us the safety spiel as we strap into our harnesses.

"I could get used to these." Caleb gestures to the harness wrapped around his waist and thighs, an obvious vee framing his groin.

"Oh, it's a very sexy look," I tease. "The women in Suitor's Crossing won't know what hit them if they see you in that getup."

"That's exactly what I'm going for... Though there's really only one woman whose opinion matters." He drops a quick kiss to my cheek before dipping his hand in a bag of chalk, removing a handful, then slapping it between his palms. A nuclear blast of dust erupts in the air, sending both of us into coughing fits.

"I don't think you're supposed to use that much," I wheeze, caught between coughing out the particles of chalk in my throat and laughing at the absurdity of the situation.

"That dude didn't warn about chalk inhalation. You'd think that would be part of their safety protocol."

"He probably thought it was common sense, since I assume most people don't grab enough chalk to scale El Capitan."

"Someone watched *Free Solo*... But I'm a newbie and can't be blamed for my mistakes." Once his breathing is under control, Caleb starts climbing, and I carefully hold his belaying rope, a little scared of letting him fall. "You good down there, Sierra Bear?"

"Yeah, just don't make any sudden movements. I don't want to slip."

"That'd be a downer. Hate to end up in the emergency room on our date. I have different plans for tonight." He looks down at me from above and winks. A flush of heat causes a light sheen of sweat to form on my skin.

I have different plans, too—ones that don't involve an ER bed but my big comfy mattress at home.

Caleb rings the bell at the top of the rock wall, and then carefully rappels back down, so we can switch spots. "Think you can beat my time?" he asks, nodding to the clock next to us that showcases how quickly he climbed the wall in red digital numbers.

This may be my first rock climbing experience, but I'm a competitive woman, especially when it comes to Caleb. Just because we've called a truce on the business rivalry doesn't mean the idea of beating him in competition has disappeared. It just makes the stakes much more interesting.

"You're on. Loser buys victory smoothies." The sound of blenders on the other side of the warehouse have been a constant background noise ever since we stepped foot into the building, and a pineapple mango smoothie will be the perfect prize for my win.

"Deal. Now, get to climbing, sweetcakes."

My concentration falls to the wall in front of me, my eyes slowly mapping a path before reaching for the first hand hold. Caleb encourages me every step of the way, but I don't waste my breath or precious time by responding. I've got the advantage of knowing the time to beat while Caleb moseyed up the wall still holding a conversation with me.

"Ten seconds!"

"Five, four, three—"

My fist snags the bell's metal clapper, ringing it for all it's worth. A couple of onlookers cheer at my victory as I push off from the rock wall in a slow descent, then Caleb embraces me in a bear hug that lifts my feet off the ground again.

"Damn, that was quite the show you put on," he whispers in my ear. "The view from below was sexy as fuck."

"Were you checking out my ass while I did my workout for the week?" I playfully slap his back but inwardly grin. He warned me to wear comfortable clothes before he picked me up tonight, so the black leggings conform to my thick thighs and round ass, leaving little to the imagination.

"Can you blame me? It's a fine ass." A chuckle vibrates in my ear as his hand lowers to cop a feel of one butt cheek before lightly smacking it. "Come on, I owe you a smoothie."

The concessions line moves quickly, and soon we're sitting on a bench watching a group of friends race across a tall set of monkey bars. "So, what do you think? Totally worth the drive to Everton, right?" Caleb sucks up more of his strawberry banana smoothie. "We're going to have to come back here again for a rematch."

"Or for a good stress reliever or workout session."

Once we've rested, we meander around the building and try out the jungle gym and a couple of the other setups before calling it a night. Fatigue settles in my muscles as soon as we're on the road to Suitor's Crossing.

I should shower and go to bed once I get home, but when Caleb parks and walks me up to my apartment door, sleep is the last thing on my mind. A second wave of energy sparks in my blood. "Want to come in for a nightcap?"

"Sure."

We step inside my living room, and I debate whether to offer a drink or suggest what I really want. *We're taking risks these days, remember?* Going with my gut, I veer away from the kitchen and towards the bathroom.

"What if I told you I lied about the nightcap, and I'd rather we did something else?"

"I'd say I'm listening..."

We're both sweaty from the climb and covered in flecks of chalk, so I tug my shirt over my head and toss it to the floor. "Then how about a hot shower to clean off?"

Caleb reciprocates and pulls his own tee over his head. "I can get behind that." Both of us grin like sex-crazed maniacs as a race ensues to see who can get naked the fastest.

Of course, Caleb wins because my stupid sports bra gets tangled up around me. "Ugh, I hate these things," I grumble.

"Me, too," he murmurs. "Me. Too." His fingers grip underneath the elastic band and maneuver it higher and higher until my breasts are free and the hot pink spandex can be thrown to the carpet. "Damn, sweetcakes. Your tits are fucking hot." He molds the large globes with his rough palms, the soft flesh overflowing his fingers.

"Mmm... That's not the only sexy part of me."

Caleb walks me back into the bathroom where I blindly reach to turn on the water for a shower. "Oh, I definitely concur." He squeezes a butt cheek. "There's your sexy smile." He kisses the corner of my mouth. "Your business acumen." His lips caress my temple. "And let's not forget your sassy attitude."

"You've got a thing for my smart mouth?" Hot water sluices off my back, and I groan at the immediate relief to my sore muscles.

"Hmm... You mean those pouty lips that drive me crazy? Yeah, I've got a thing for them. For you." He kisses up my neck. "You're the whole package, sweetcakes, and I can't wait to make you mine."

"No one's stopping you."

"Not anymore, you mean." Caleb rears back to give me a pointed look, and I roll my eyes.

"Yeah, yeah, yeah... I'm the one who kept our feud going. Whatever." My nails dig into his shoulders. "Are you going to chastise me for all these years we missed out on? Or are you finally gonna fuck me?"

A devilish smirk ghosts across his face. "Ah, there's that smart mouth I know and love."

Love.

Why doesn't that word bother me like it should?

CHAPTER ELEVEN

CALEB

Did I really think Sierra would let me fuck her tonight after our date?

No.

Had I been hopeful?

Hell, yes.

Slick curves slide beneath my roaming hands after I pour a dollop of her body wash into my palm, the scent of vanilla rising in the steaming air. It's arousing as fuck.

Her signature scent teases my nose. But if I'm honest, everything about Sierra is a tease.

I nuzzle into the cleavage of her breasts and pray one day I get to fuck them. Like a dream I had the other night.

"Caleb..." she hums in pleasure, her smaller hands caressing my back and sides before digging into my abs. My thumbs flick her nipples—entranced by the stiffening buds—and their lure is too strong as I suck one and then the other into my mouth, playing with the sensitive tips with my teeth until her hand wraps around my dick and tugs.

"*Fuck.* Not going to last long with you squeezing my dick like that."

"Now, Caleb, don't disappoint me before we've even gotten started." She smirks then lowers to her knees. A soapy waterfall drips down her curvy body, and the caveman inside me wants to add my release to the mix.

"I just warned you about my current predicament, so you decide you're gonna suck me off in response?"

Sierra shrugs and the water cascades down her round shoulders. "What can I say? I've been wanting to know the feel of your thick cock in my mouth since that night in your Jeep when it kept digging into my thigh."

"Well, I'm not gonna stop you, if that's what you really want." Who was I to question her needs?

Her twinkling green eyes stare up at me before her lashes flutter closed and her lips suction around the dripping head of my cock. Moaning vibrations travel up the stiff length, up my spine, and straight to my head until I'm dizzy with the need for relief.

My hands fall to the tiles behind her. A swirl of her tongue. The strong pull from her lips. Her hands kneading my ass. They all work together until I come with a shout.

"Goddamn, you're good at that..." I groan, dragging in a lungful of steamy air. "You know, I'm good, too."

"At sucking dick?" Sierra laughs at the twisted expression on my face.

"No, smartass. At eating pussy." We switch positions, so I'm the one on my knees, her back to the wall. I lift one of her legs so it's draped over my shoulder, widening her stance so I have an unobstructed view of her pink cunt.

"You have no right to be this goddamn pretty," I growl.

No man could resist such temptation, and certainly not me.

Diving forward, my tongue plunges deep inside her channel as my thumb circles her clit. Her hips grind against me, shoving her pussy so close I can barely breathe, but what a way to go. "Come on, sweetcakes. Come for me. I know you want to."

And damn, but I want it to.

To have her sweet release coating my beard and her cries of pleasure ringing in my ears.

I stroke her pussy with my fingers, finding that special spot within as I shift to suck on her clit. A second later, her orgasm scorches my cheeks, and I lower to lap at the gush of honeyed arousal.

"Mmm... that's a good girl. A curvy little treat just for me." I continue to lick and suck her sensitive folds, unable to stop, until she whimpers and starts pushing at my head, silently begging for no more.

"Wow, we really should have done that years ago," she pants, melting like jello in my arms.

"At least we can make up for lost time," I promise. Reaching around her, I turn off the shower, towel us both off, and run a brush through Sierra's hair as quickly but as gently as I can before carrying her to bed.

Tucking her soft body into my chest with the comforter covering our shoulders, I wait for a response from Sierra.

All I get is a soft snore.

Guess I wore my girl out tonight.

And I couldn't be happier about it as sleep claims me as well.

"SO, YOU AND SIERRA, huh? About damn time. You've been circling each other for forever." Cole leans back in his chair across from me at The Ole Aces, where we decided to meet up for a beer.

"Blame Sierra for the drawn out theatrics. I'm just glad she finally gave me an opportunity to see past all those cannons, archers, and stone walls she erected in my path."

"Yeah, but in a weird way, you kind of loved it. Going head to head with her."

"True, but I like this side of things way more." Just thinking about our night together, remembering the taste of her pussy, has me shifting uncomfortably in my seat.

I need a repeat performance. Stat.

Unfortunately, it's been all hands on deck with the renovation and business plans. Every evening Sierra and I end up being too exhausted to do much more than kiss goodnight and fall asleep from exhaustion.

It fucking sucks being a responsible adult on the far side of thirty-five.

"I bet you do." Cole slaps my back in amusement before asking how things are going otherwise, and I appreciate the reprieve.

I'd hate to have to walk out of here with an erection the size of a baseball bat hindering me. And that's what will happen if we continue to talk about Sierra.

Even if the conversation isn't inherently sexy, *she is*.

So I ramble on about my parents' upcoming cruise to Alaska and force my thoughts toward glaciers and grizzly bears rather than a certain curvy baker who drives me to distraction.

CHAPTER TWELVE

SIERRA

The morning of the All Schools Day parade dawns bright and early, and I hit the ground running. Caleb and I need to set up our booth at the community building where everyone congregates after the parade, plus finalize any last-minute details before the grand opening of Crossing's Cups & Cakes.

It's crazy to me that the day we've been preparing for is finally here. Not too long ago I was caught sneaking into my arch nemesis's coffee shop and now I've joined forces with him to create a revamped bakery and coffee shop combination. Brewed no longer exists, neither does Buttercream Dreams, and in their place is Crossing's Cups & Cakes.

Shrugging on a hoodie with our updated logo, I grab my keys and bag before heading out the door and driving to our newly renovated location. Construction finished a few days ago and we spent the intervening time between then and now organizing tables, chairs, and decor. After our grand reveal today at the parade, we will officially be open to a crowd of customers.

"Ready, Sierra Bear?" Caleb looks up from his laptop once I step into the back office we're sharing.

"Ready as I'll ever be." My stuff clanks to the desktop next to an iced coffee and blueberry muffin. "What's this?" I ask before greedily sucking down the sugary goodness.

"Your favorite drink and breakfast treat. Figured we should start the day off on a high note."

The thoughtful gesture surprises me even if it shouldn't. Ever since our picnic date, Caleb has shown me a totally different side of himself. He still likes to play pranks and knows how to rile me up, but my perspective has changed. It's playful rather than malicious—although the more I think about it the more I doubt any of his actions were meant to be malicious in the first place. They were all misinterpretations in my head. Shannon would say it was my overdramatic side getting the best of me.

"Thanks. Is everything ready for us to transport? Or do I need to start—"

Caleb shakes his head. "Nope, we're good. It was smart to finish everything last night, so this morning goes easier. Let's load up my Jeep, then we can get going. Mandy's still coming in after the parade, right?"

"Yep, she'll man the store while we're in the booth."

"And Tristan will help her," Caleb adds, mentioning one of his baristas. "With Keely on standby, if they need more help."

"Fingers crossed they do!" I want today to be huge for our opening, especially after all the hard work we've put into it.

The morning passes quickly with table set-up and chatting with our booth neighbors, and soon we're waiting restlessly for parade-goers to arrive. The only downside to the day so far is our competitor being placed in a booth right across from us. Someone dressed as a cappuccino dances in front of their table while a guy wearing a polo urges people to spin a giant wheel for a prize.

"We should have thought of something like that," I lament. Hell, even I'd want to spin that wheel like a contestant on *Wheel of Fortune*, and those guys are technically the enemy. No way the families that pass are going to be able to resist—not with little kid hands instinctively reaching for one of the fun prizes.

"Let them give away cheap plastic toys." Caleb nudges my shoulder. "They can afford it, but we don't need to waste our money on gimmicks."

"I hope you're right. Everybody likes free stuff."

"We've got free treats," he reminds me.

It's funny how optimistic he is. And kind of endearing. But lately I've found a lot of Caleb's traits attractive, a strange twist on how I previously viewed him.

"Hey guys, this looks great." Shannon and Cole approach our booth as the sound of a band outside wails in the background. One of the marching bands must have decided to provide people with an encore.

"Thanks. This is our moment of truth. Whether or not we totally fucked up our businesses, or if combining was a good choice."

"It's a good choice. A smart one." Shannon comforts me again. She's heard me go back and forth on this for the past couple of weeks. Like a broken record, I'm sure I've driven her crazy with my worries.

"Yeah, it's not like the two of you disappeared. Your businesses are still the same. Just in one convenient location," Cole interjects, offering a closed fist for Caleb to pound with his own in greeting.

"That's what I've been telling her. But Sierra likes to worry."

"No kidding." Shannon laughs. "We'll catch you guys later, okay? Willow is here with Rhys somewhere at a booth for his custom ironwork, and I'm curious to see it all displayed."

After agreeing to meet up for dinner, Caleb and I turn on the smiles and greet everyone who passes by. A blur of new and familiar faces, all excited about Crossing's Cups & Cakes, form a constant line around us, and every so often Caleb catches my eye and winks or smiles or mouths some kind of encouragement. In general, crowds don't bother me, but with the stress of launching something new, meeting so many people can be overwhelming. Caleb's calm presence and attention helps ground me in a way I didn't expect.

People compliment our new name, the cute rebranding, the updated coffee and pastry flavors. All in all, it's been the best launch I could have imagined. And I'm grateful for Luna suggesting the idea. For Caleb pushing me to accept it.

"YOU'RE AMAZING, YOU know?"

"I do," I say with a grin. After an exhausting day, we're both leaning against the Crossing's Cups & Cakes counter looking out the front windows at a glowing Main Street. Leftover candy and confetti—remnants from the earlier parade—litter the sidewalk where the garbage patrol missed some spots. "But why exactly am I amazing today?"

"You're great with customers, as expected, and you've really trusted me these past few months. Something I never thought you would do, but I'm grateful for it."

"It's easier to trust you when we're working towards a common goal."

"True." He laughs. "Have you thought about us anymore? Since our date, our relationship has kind of been on the backburner because of how hectic it's been around here. But things aren't going to slow down anytime soon." Caleb faces me and cups my cheek. "If we want this to work, we'll need to make time for it."

He's right. Ever since our date and that amazing night together, I've been thinking about what our future holds. Dating my business partner. Falling in love with my former enemy. And today helped me remember what good can come from taking a leap of faith.

"I agree." I turn my head to plant a kiss in the center of his palm. "We may have started out rocky—mostly because of me and my theatrics." I roll my eyes heavenward at the bark of laughter he tries to disguise as a cough. "But even when I referred to you as my arch nemesis, I still had this pesky attraction to the guy next door."

"Pesky?" Caleb mock frowns and slaps my ass before hooking me around the waist and tugging me closer.

"Yep. How could I have a thing for my enemy? The guy who drove me crazy? It wasn't rational."

"It's hot. Everyone falls for the villain these days."

"You're not a villain. You're the push I needed to break out of my rut. A rut I didn't even realize I was in until you made me see it. So, thanks."

"You're very welcome, sweetcakes." Caleb takes a deep breath then slowly exhales, his tender gaze studying mine. "Thank *you* for trusting me and giving me a chance. I promise you won't regret it."

"Oh, I'm sure I'll regret it sometimes. You can be very annoying when you want to be," I tease.

"You make it so easy."

"Yeah, yeah, yeah. Just kiss me already."

"You don't have to tell me twice." He presses a hard kiss to my lips, and I follow his mouth when he retreats, hoping for something a little longer, a little more passionate, which is when my frustrating but endearing man suggests, "Let's have a quickie in celebration for our first day in business."

At first, I think he's kidding, but then Caleb drags me back to our office, away from the front window where anyone driving by could see us.

"This is so unprofessional." But I don't fight him when he unbuttons my jeans. Or rips my CCC tee off. Not even when he bends me over his desk, my palms clinging to the edges of the heavy oak.

"You okay, sweetcakes?" Caleb pauses with the head of his cock at my soaking entrance, waiting for my consent.

"More than okay." I rock my hips back in a silent plea. "Don't stop now. We were just getting to the good part."

A rumble of amusement vibrates against my back before the swift thrust of his cock burying deep steals my breath. Holy hell, I knew he'd feel good, but damn... The stretch of his thick length pummeling in and out of my pussy is more than I imagined.

My hands search for something, *anything*, to grasp for purchase. To anchor me to Earth rather than shooting straight into the sky like a bottle rocket.

Caleb licks a wet trail up my neck to whisper in my ear. "You're mine, Sierra. This cunt is made for me. *You* are made for me."

"Yes..."

"And you're going to come for me, aren't you? You're going to come for your man because this little pussy can't get enough of my dick." He grunts and curses, his rhythm increasing. Drilling me into the desk like he wants a permanent imprint of my body on the dark wood.

Wouldn't that be a sight for visitors to our office? But I can't find it in me to care as my pleasure peaks, and I collapse under Caleb's weight.

It may be nice to have a reminder of tonight. The grand opening of our business. The grand christening of our relationship.

"My sweet Sierra Bear." Caleb nuzzles my cheek, and I sigh, hopeful for the future.

Maybe I don't hate that nickname, after all.

EPILOGUE

CALEB

YEARS LATER

"Mom! Dad's messing with my recipe again!" Nine-year-old Stella shouts from her position at the kitchen island, and I raise my hands like a perp caught red handed on an episode of *COPS*.

Sierra ambles into our family kitchen with our two-year-old Mason on her hip, amused gaze sweeping across the counter full of mixing bowls and ingredients for Stella's World-Famous Snickerdoodles—or at least, Suitor's Crossing-famous. Like mother like daughter, our oldest has a knack for baking, though I still try to add my flair every once and while. To little success.

"What's he done now, honey?"

Stella wrinkles her nose and tips the stainless steel bowl in her hands forward. "He dumped coffee grounds into my cookie batter."

"You said I could help," I say, tugging on one of her pigtails.

"With mixing because my arm gets tired."

"Go easy on your dad, Stell. He just can't help himself." Sierra rounds the island to lean against my side. "He's never gotten over the fact that I beat him all those years ago at Pastry Palooza, so he's still trying to prove his baking skills. Isn't that right?"

"Both of you said you liked my coffee snickerdoodles last month. I figured I'd spice things up again."

"Oh, my sweet summer child... They tasted fine, but you can't beat Stella's World-Famous recipe." Sierra pats my cheek then Stella copies her mom by gently tapping my arm. My girls giggle at the aggrieved sigh I release, though I'm not bothered by their teasing. It's one of the highlights of my life making the two of them laugh anyway I can, even if it's at my expense.

"Alright, alright. Point taken. I'll finish this batch of cookies while you start a fresh one, Stella. Maybe we should have a Pastry Palooza 2.0—Father vs Daughter, hosted at Crossing's Cups & Cakes. What do you think?"

Another laugh bursts from Sierra and Mason's childish squeal follows. "I don't think your ego could handle losing to a nine-year-old. Because my girl would kick your butt. Right, Stella?"

"Right!" Our daughter dumps the 'ruined' cookie batter in front of me before grabbing a clean bowl and measuring her dry ingredients all over again. I love watching her concentrate and flit around the kitchen, just like her mom. Their mannerisms are exactly alike. A mini-Sierra. Sass and all.

And I wouldn't trade our little family for anything.

Not for Sierra and I's old rivalry. Not for my old coffee shop, Brewed.

Our business and relationship turned out just the way it was intended, even if it took a while for the *heart sparks* to work their magic. The important part is that in the end I got my soul mate, my feisty Sierra Bear—the perfect partner for me.

Continue reading for a sneak peek into the next book in the *Hearts Collide* series, *Hidden Hearts*, featuring Avery from Design Time!

CHAPTER ONE

AVERY MONAGHAN

A piercing ring breaks the silence as I grab my lunch from the small refrigerator in the corner of the room. Since we're a small family-owned business, there isn't much space allotted for a break room, so most of the time, I pull my lunch from the fridge only to eat in my car or at the conference table near the front of the store.

Ignoring my growling stomach, I pick up the cordless phone and hit the blinking green button. "Design Time. This is Avery."

"Mike, please." An abrupt male voice comes over the line.

"May I ask who's calling?" I set down the baggies containing my sandwich and baby carrots and reach for a pen, ready to write down his information.

"Dominic."

I roll my eyes at the one-word answer. Everyone expects my boss to know who they are—failing to realize that there are a million other Johns, Sarahs, and Toms out in the world.

"And who are you with?" I prompt, digging for more information, knowing Mike will want to know before accepting the call. He's forced me to switch back and forth between him and previous callers before to gather pertinent details in pieces, rather than him just taking the call and finding out for himself.

Reason #47 for why I'm itching to quit this job.

"Will you just put Mike on the phone? He'll know who I am." The man's getting disgruntled now, and all I can think is *join the club, buddy*.

Because these kinds of calls are the worst. I guarantee you are not as memorable as you think you are, and now you're forcing me to basically interrogate you. Always a fun task when dealing with a frustrated stranger on the other end of the line. If I liked pestering people with personal questions, I would've joined the FBI instead of winding up here.

"Well, just in case, what company are you with?"

"I don't have time for this. Are you going to get him or not?" Shocker. This guy is rude and arrogant—a winning combination from hell.

"Just a second." Fed up, I page Mike. "There's a Dominic on the phone. He won't say who he's with, but he's getting upset, so you might want to talk to him."

Mike sighs over the phone. "Fine."

And just like that the line is picked up, and I don't have to handle Mr. Rude Caller anymore. I throw up a mental image of the middle finger to entitled customers everywhere then grab my lunch and book it out of here before something else keeps me from my break.

When I walked into Design Time four years ago, I was looking for a graphic design position. Graduation was coming quickly, and I needed a job.

I figured a custom screen printing and embroidery company could use another designer considering the demand in our small town—a demand I'd witnessed throughout college with numerous orders for athletic team apparel, staff shirts, and the like.

I even accepted that I'd be expected to pitch in to help with the retail side of the store, since I'd be fresh out of college with no prior professional experience. For the longest time, I chalked up my frustrations to paying my dues—that if I just waited a little longer, I'd be promoted to where I wanted to be.

However, that dream has gotten further and further away as the years have passed, and it's obvious my path will never take that direction, at least not here. Which is why I've been saving for over a year in preparation for leaving Design Time.

Fortunately, living in a small town like Suitor's Crossing and having no social life has allowed me to save a sizable nest egg. All that really holds me back now is figuring out where to go and what to do. After all this time, I'm not even sure I qualify as a graphic designer anymore, or if that's where my passion lies, since I haven't kept up with the latest software and design trends.

After lunch, I return to stitching the logo of a local grain company on a large order of caps when Mike enters the workroom, interrupting my thoughts about the future. I have a terrible habit of daydreaming while working, since it doesn't require much thinking once the embroidery machines are set correctly.

A bad habit considering the number of times my poor fingers have been nicked by needles.

Change can't come soon enough.

"Next time Dominic Stone calls, put him through. He's interested in renting one of my commercial properties," Mike says as he stops beside me, looking over my shoulder to study the pattern the needles are creating. His micromanaging has improved over the years, and truthfully, he gives me more leniency than the other embroiderer, Tony. But his hovering still makes me nervous.

"Will do!" I chirp, hoping he returns to his office soon.

Mike has a lot of different business ventures, so I field a fair share of calls about available rentals. A while back I thought with the added responsibility of managing this store that he might include me in his other businesses as a more personal assistant type. While not my dream job, it's something I enjoy, and at least it would be something different to keep my interest.

But it's never come up, and if I'm honest, I don't want to get more entrenched here than I already am. It's going to be hard enough to quit, something I'm still working up the courage to do. Not because I'm second-guessing my decision, but because I hate letting people down.

Mike gave me a chance after college, and despite my issues with his managing style and the job, there's still a sense of loyalty to him and Design Time. Which makes my choice to leave feel more personal than it should be.

It's just business, I remind myself. *You have to do what's best for you.*

Easier said than done.

Find the rest of Avery and Dominic's story in book two of the *Hearts Collide* series, *Hidden Hearts*!

THANKS FOR READING & DON'T FORGET TO RATE/ REVIEW!

Please consider leaving a rating/review. Ratings & reviews are the #1 way to support an indie author like me.
The more reviews, the more my books are shown to other potential readers!
And they serve as guides to readers on whether or not to take a chance on an indie author.
I appreciate your support!
XO, Hallie

ABOUT THE AUTHOR

Hallie prefers steamy, insta-love stories where curvy girls are claimed by filthy-talking heroes. And when she ran out of reading material, she decided to write her own stories. If you want a quick, hot read, she's your girl!

www.ingramcontent.com/pod-product-compliance
Lightning Source LLC
Chambersburg PA
CBHW030356180626
46812CB00007B/2906